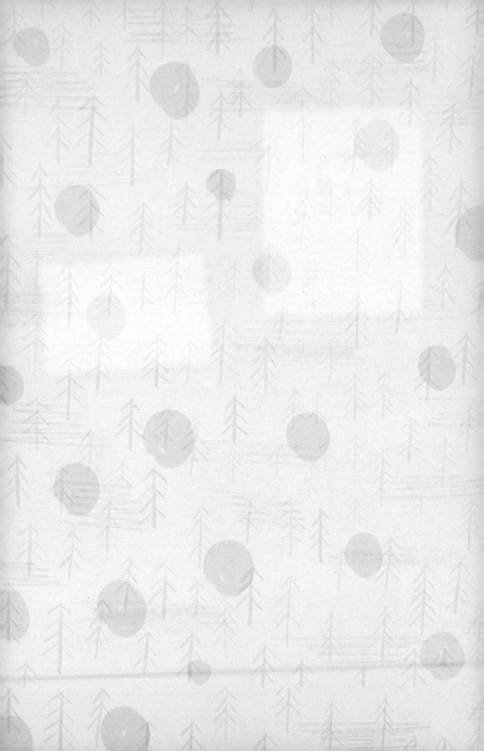

THE
MISSING
BOOKSHOP

For all my fellow indie booksellers — Katie

To Linda and Dave Drayton, my
mammar and pops, for instilling a love
of reading and books in me — Kirsti

First American Edition 2019
Kane Miller, A Division of EDC Publishing

Text copyright © Katie Clapham, 2019
Illustrations copyright © Kirsti Beautyman, 2019

First published in Great Britain in 2019 by Stripes Publishing Ltd,
an imprint of the Little Tiger Group

For information contact:
Kane Miller, A Division of EDC Publishing
P.O. Box 470663
Tulsa, OK 74147-0663

www.kanemiller.com
www.edcpub.com
www.usbornebooksandmore.com

Library of Congress Control Number: 2018958220

Printed and bound in China.
STP/1800/0377/0920

2 4 6 8 10 9 7 5 3

ISBN: 978-1-61067-901-5

THE
MISSING
BOOKSHOP

Katie
Clapham

Kirsti
Beautyman

Kane Miller
A DIVISION OF EDC PUBLISHING

"The End,"

Mrs. Minty said as she closed the
book and smiled at the children
on the rainbow carpet.

"Thank you for coming to story time, and I hope to see you all next week."

Milly never missed story time at Minty's Bookshop. Mrs. Minty knew about every book in the whole world. Milly liked to give her challenges.

"One with pirates!"

"One with a bear in it!"

"Ponies?"

"Aliens!"

Mrs. Minty always
had just the thing.

"So, Milly," said Mom, coming over. "Have you decided?"

Today was a special day because Milly had saved enough pocket money to buy a book.

"I think I'd like some sort of

sea adventure,"

Milly replied excitedly.

"Aha!" said Mrs. Minty. "I have

just the thing!"

Mrs. Minty got up from her creaky wooden story chair.

"Goodness! I'm getting a bit creaky, too!"
she said. She smiled, but Milly couldn't help
noticing how slowly she walked.

Mrs. Minty trailed her fingers along one of the
shelves and pulled out a book with a turquoise
cover and gold writing.

"I think you'll like this," she said,
her eyes twinkling. "It's full of mermaids
and sea monsters."

Milly took the book and opened it at the first page.

"Hang on, Milly,"
Mom called.

"We need to pay for it first! Why don't you
tidy up the story area while I find your
pocket money for Mrs. Minty?"

Milly handed her mom the book and went to
gather up the colorful cushions.

The colors didn't look that bright anymore.

She turned one over to see if the other side looked
better, but that was all worn, too.

Looking around the bookshop, she
could see that the paint was starting to
peel off around the window frames,
and the curtains were faded.

But it still looked sort of marvelous because it was filled with

shelves and shelves

of wonderful
books.

Milly glanced over at the picture
of Mrs. Minty and her daughter
sitting on the wooden story chair
when it was brand new.

Mrs. Minty looked quite different now.

In the picture, Mrs. Minty didn't
have her little reading glasses,
and her long silver hair was as
red as an apple.

"Time to go, Milly,"
her mom called.

As Milly left the bookshop, a little worry
cloud formed above her head.

Mrs. Minty, her wooden story chair, and her whole bookshop were all getting a bit creaky.

Milly and her mom always popped into the café after story time. But today Milly couldn't concentrate on her new book. Or her strawberry smoothie.

"What do you do if something is old and creaky?" she asked her mom.

"Well, you have to treat it very carefully, so it doesn't break. But eventually it might need replacing with something new," Milly's mom said, sipping her tea.

Milly was shocked.

Mrs. Minty couldn't be replaced!

That night Milly looked at her bookshelves. They were filled with books from Minty's Bookshop: funny stories of children making mischief, exotic tales of old kings, amazing atlases, picture books, and books of poems. Mrs. Minty had helped her choose every one.

The bookshop could never close!
Milly snuggled under her duvet. Perhaps if everyone
looked after it, it wouldn't break, and it wouldn't
need to be replaced. As she fell asleep, Milly thought
about all the things she could do to help.

At story time the following week, Milly was extra helpful.

She chose the comfiest cushion for Mrs. Minty's story chair.

She laid out the cushions for the other children...

...and she tidied them
all away at the end.

She even helped one boy
find a copy of the book Mrs.
Minty had been reading from.

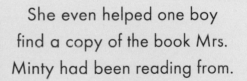

"You'd make a wonderful
bookseller, Milly!"
Mrs. Minty joked.

But was it a joke? Milly couldn't help wondering.

Did Mrs. Minty
want her to run the
bookshop?

Milly thought working in a bookshop might be the best grown-up job there could be, but she wasn't a grown-up yet!

Milly watched Mrs. Minty helping a customer.

"I'm looking for a book for my nephew.
He plays cricket," a lady was saying.

"We've got lots
of books about cricket,"
said Mrs. Minty.

"And a book for my niece – she just got
a pet bearded dragon!"

"I'll have to order it,
but I know just the
thing."

Mrs. Minty was a walking encyclopedia when it came to books. How could Milly ever learn to be like that?

As Milly followed Mom up the road, her worry cloud grew a little heavier.

Milly gasped. If nobody else wanted to run Minty's it might be replaced by a bank or an optician.

What use were glasses
if there were no books to read?

If Mrs. Minty could just stay until Milly was grown up and had become an encyclopedia of books...

Milly leaped to her feet.

"Can we go back to
the bookshop, Mom?
There's something
I need to tell
Mrs. Minty."

Milly's mom waited outside while Milly
raced back inside the shop.

"Mrs. Minty!" she called out.
"Mrs. Minty!

"I just needed to tell you
that ... banks are very boring and
bookshops are very important.
I love your shop. I love coming to story
time, but I want to sit on the rainbow carpet
and **not on the wooden story chair.**
I'd **love** to work here one day, but
I'm not an encyclopedia yet, and
**Minty's Bookshop can
never be replaced!"**

It all came out so fast and
jumbled up. Mrs. Minty looked
rather surprised.

"Well, Milly, thank you. I think
I agree with everything you
said." She smiled. "If you keep
coming to story time, I'll keep
telling the stories. How's that?"

"Just the thing," Milly said,
and they both laughed.

Milly's worry cloud almost disappeared over the weekend. After school on Monday they headed to the bookshop as usual.

But the

bookshop

was

closed.

"That's odd! I'm sure Mrs. Minty would've told us if she was going away," Mom said as Milly peered through the locked door. There was no sign of Mrs. Minty and no notice on the door to say when she'd be back.

"I hope she's all right!" Mom said. But even she looked worried. "How about a smoothie?" she suggested.

But Milly shook her head. There was no way she could enjoy a smoothie today.

35

They checked
the shop
after school
every day.

The following
week there
was a sign
that said...

CLOSED
DUE TO
UNFORESEEN
CIRCUMSTANCES

...which Milly's mom said meant that something had happened that no one had planned.

The week after
that, it said...

CLOSED
UNTIL
FURTHER
NOTICE

...which meant that
no one knew when it
would be open again.

The week after that, Milly and her mom found a van outside the shop. It was filled with things from the bookshop. The rainbow carpet was rolled up. The faded cushions were piled on top of each other.

The dusty picture frames were lying in a heap.
And Mrs. Minty's wooden story chair was upside
down on top of a cardboard box.

A tall lady with her hair tied up in a spotty scarf
came out of the bookshop and closed the van door.

She got into the driver's seat and drove away
before Milly had a chance to say anything.

Mom took Milly's
hand, and they walked
up to the café.

But even a slice of
strawberry cake couldn't
help Milly shake the sad
feeling in her tummy.

Mrs. Minty had
gone, and it looked
like her bookshop
was going to be
replaced.

The next time they saw it, the bookshop was boarded up, and the sign said "For Sale."

Milly's mom said that meant things were going to change.

FOR
SALE
CALL: 0020412

It was a wet weekend. Milly usually loved wet weekends. It meant she could sit on her window seat reading without Mom telling her to go outside.

But today the words seemed to swim in front of her eyes.

Mom came in with a mug of hot chocolate. "What are you reading, Milly?"

Milly showed her the cover. It was a story about a girl who loved books, and it was one of her all-time favorites.

"*Matilda*!" Her mom smiled. "Haven't you read that one a million times?"

"Yes, but it makes me feel better when I feel sad."

"Oh dear. Is it because of Mrs. Minty?" Mom asked, sitting down next to her.

Milly closed the book and
snuggled into her mom.

"I can't stop thinking about her! Where has
she gone? Why is the shop closed? Who is
changing it, and what will they change it to?"

"Oh Milly, these are all good questions, but
I don't have the answers, I'm afraid."

Milly could feel tears in her eyes. "Do you
think Minty's could be replaced by
another bookshop?"

"I hope so, Milly," her mom said, picking up
Matilda. "Now, where did you get to?"
They took turns reading the last few chapters aloud.
Matilda had a very happy ending. It always did.

"Try not to worry, Milly," her mom said
as she tucked her into bed that night.
"We'll find out what happened to
Mrs. Minty, I promise."

Milly tried to fall asleep. She tried to think of nice places where Mrs. Minty could be.

Maybe she was reading a book on a deserted island...

Or sitting by a lake...

Or sipping a coffee in a busy city...

But why would she suddenly go away
without telling anyone?

By Sunday afternoon Milly had come up with a plan. Wherever Mrs. Minty was, it was up to Milly to find someone to run the bookshop for her. Someone who loved books. Someone who knew how much the town needed a bookshop. Someone who could see Minty's the way she saw it... And she knew just what to do.

She got her crayons and began to draw the bookshop – not as it looked today, but as she imagined it looked when it first opened.

With bright-yellow paint, flowers in the window boxes, and a beautiful window display. The red door was wide open, showing a hint of the books inside. It looked amazing.

On the way home from school on Monday,
Milly asked her mom to help her stick her picture
to the boarded-up bookshop.

"It's a wonderful picture, Milly," said
Mom. "I know Mrs. Minty would love it."

Milly smiled. Mrs. Minty would love it,
but Milly needed whoever was going to
buy the shop to love it, too.

On **Tuesday**, there was another picture
stuck to the boards next to Milly's.

It was a drawing of Mrs. Minty on her
wooden story chair.

On Wednesday,
someone had added
a note. It said:

we miss
you, minty's
BOOKSHOP

On **Thursday**, there was a poem. Milly's mom read it to her.

AN ODE TO
MINTY'S

BOOKSHOPS ARE WONDERFUL
BOOKSHOPS ARE GREAT
BUT MRS MINTYS BOOKSHOP
IS MY VERY FAVOURITE
PLACE!
THE BEST STORYTIMES
AND ALWAYS LOTS OF
LAUGHTER, A
DAY SPENT IN MINTYS
IS A HAPPY EVER AFTER!

It was called **"An Ode to Minty's,"**
which she said meant it was all about how
much the writer loved the bookshop.

On **Friday**, there were too many
new things to count. Drawings,
letters and photographs were stuck
all around Milly's picture.

There was no way the new owners could ignore this.

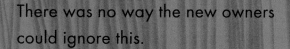

AN ODE TO MINTY'S

BOOKSHOPS ARE WONDERFUL
BOOKSHOPS ARE GREAT
BUT MRS MINTYS BOOKSHOP
IS MY VERY FAVOURITE
PLACE!
THE BEST STORYTIMES
AND ALWAYS LOTS OF
LAUGHTER. A
DAY SPENT IN MINTYS
IS A HAPPY EVER AFTER!

SAVE OUR BOOK SHOP

The weekend brought
warm sunshine. Milly
was sitting in her
neighbor's garden
while her mom was at
the supermarket.

She was reading about the Egyptians when her mom came rushing through the back door still carrying the shopping.

"Milly! There's a new sign at the bookshop! And guess what? It says a new bookshop will be opening in one week!"

It was a long week.

Every time Milly and her mom passed the bookshop, Milly couldn't help peeping through the gaps in the boards.

More notes and pictures had been added.

Someone had started a countdown.

4 DAYS TO GO!

5 DAYS TO GO

DAYS TO GO!

2 DAYS

1 DAY

The night before
the grand opening,
Milly could
hardly sleep.

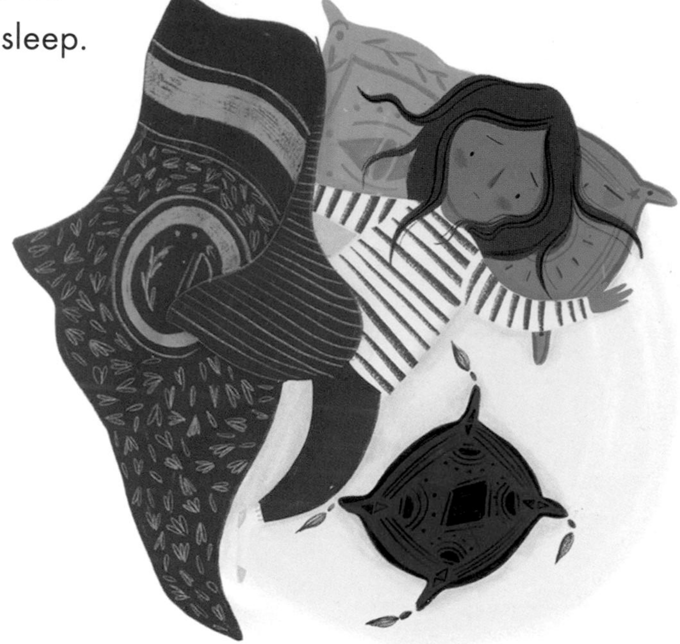

She couldn't wait
to visit the new
bookshop.

But she couldn't stop thinking about Mrs. Minty, too.

What had happened to her?

And could Milly learn to love the new owners of the bookshop?

On Saturday morning, Milly danced by the front door, desperate to get going.

"There's no need to race," her mom laughed, as they set off. "It's open all day!"

As the bookshop came into view, Milly
couldn't believe her eyes.

It looked exactly like her drawing!

The paint was the same sunflower yellow.
The window boxes were filled with flowers.
There were balloons and bunting in among the
window displays. And through the open door she
could see shelves and shelves of books.

"Welcome to Minty's Bookshop!"

It was the lady with the spotty scarf!

"It's still Minty's!" Milly couldn't help shouting out.
Mom squeezed her hand.

"It sure is. Allow me to introduce myself – I'm Mo Minty. I'm Mrs. Minty's daughter."

Milly was a little confused. Mo Minty was the little girl in the photograph. How could she be the tall lady in the spotty scarf?

"But you're all grown up!" Milly said.

"Well, I am on the outside, but I still love children's books – in fact my favorite book of all time is *Matilda*. Have you read it?"

"I love *Matilda*!" Milly grinned, already certain that she could learn to love Mo Minty.

"But wait... Where is Mrs. Minty?" Milly asked.

"She's right over there."

Milly spun around, and there was Mrs. Minty, sitting in her newly painted wooden chair, ready to begin story time.

Milly's worry cloud burst open, and a happy feeling rained down over her.

Mrs. Minty and her bookshop were back.

She ran through the bookshop and threw her arms around Mrs. Minty.

"I've been so worried about you," she said.

"Oh Milly, I am sorry," said Mrs. Minty, "I had a fall, and I went to stay with Mo while I got better. Mo wanted me to move in with her. She even came back here to collect my things and put the shop up for sale."

Mo took over the story. "But then something amazing happened. I came over to tidy the shop after we'd packed everything up, and I saw the picture...

"It was a beautiful drawing of the bookshop just as I remembered it when I was little. I knew how special it was to me, and suddenly the thought of it closing made me very sad."

"But that was MY drawing!" cried Milly.

Mrs. Minty chuckled. "I had a feeling it was. So now Mo's moving here instead, to run the bookshop."

"With Mom's help of course. No one knows more about books than her!" added Mo.

"She's an encyclopedia of books," Milly agreed.

"Are you talking about my mommy?"
a little girl in a spotty dress said.

"No, Tilly, we're talking about Granny!" said Mo.

"Well, you know a lot about books, too,
Mommy," said Tilly. "And so do I," she added.

Mo laughed. "Milly, this is my daughter Tilly – short for Matilda."

"Milly knows a lot about books, too," said Mrs. Minty. "She never misses a story time."

"Do you want to sit next to me?" Tilly said, reaching out and holding Milly's hand.

"One day I'll run the bookshop, but I'm too little now. You could help me if you like."

"Milly and Tilly's Bookshop! I like the sound of that!" Mo laughed.

"Maybe after story time with Granny, you girls could draw a picture of your own bookshop for our wall..."

Mo pointed to a brand-new display on the wall.
It was all of the notes, photos, poems, and letters
that had been stuck to the builders' boards,
each in their own colored frame.

I ♥ MI_NTYS BOOKSHOP

I ♥ BOOKS

MISS J. Minty's OKSHOP

And in the very center, in a big sunflower-yellow wooden frame, was Milly's drawing.